Library of Congress Cataloging-in-Publication Data

McCourt, Lisa.
    Chicken soup for little souls : the best night out with Dad / story adaptation by Lisa McCourt ; illustrations by Bert Dodson.
        p.   cm.
    "Based on the . . . best-selling series Chicken soup for the soul by Jack Canfield and Mark Victor Hansen."
    Summary: When he realizes that little Vincent's father can't afford to pay for circus tickets, Danny must decide whether to share his tickets or to use them himself.
    ISBN 1-55874-508-4 (hardcover)
    [1. Sharing—Fiction. 2. Kindness—Fiction. 3. Circus—Fiction. 4. Christian life—Fiction.]
    I. Dodson, Bert, ill. II. Canfield, Jack, date. Chicken soup for the soul. III. Title.
    PZ7.M47841445Ch   1997
    [E]—dc21   97-19960
                                                                            CIP
                                                                            AC

©1997 Health Communications, Inc.
ISBN 1-55874-508-4

Story adapted from "The Circus" by Dan Clark, *A 2nd Helping of Chicken Soup for the Soul*™, edited by Jack Canfield and Mark Victor Hansen.

Story Adaptation ©1997 Lisa McCourt
Illustrations ©1997 Bert Dodson

Cover Design by Cheryl Nathan

Produced by Boingo Books, Inc.

Publisher: Health Communications, Inc.
             3201 S.W. 15th Street
             Deerfield Beach, FL 33442-8190

Printed in Mexico

For Mike McCourt, a dad who knows how to make best nights.
—L.M.

For Sydney, Riley, and Emily.
—B.D.

In memory of S. Wayne Clark.
"Any male can be a father, but it takes a special man to be a dad."
I miss you, Dad.
—D.C.

"You mean you've never been to the circus before?" Danny asked the big-eyed little kid.

The boy reached for his dad's hand, looked down, and shook his head no.

Danny was sorry he'd said it like that. The boy's clothes were mended and his sneakers were almost worn through. *Maybe his family couldn't ever afford the circus before,* Danny thought.

Danny was wearing the sweatshirt his dad had bought him the last time they went to the circus. It was his favorite shirt, with a big picture of Thor, the famous circus tiger, on it. That's what the little kid had noticed. That's why he had asked Danny what the circus was like.

"What's your name?" Danny asked him.

"Vincent," said the boy, smiling again.

"Well, Vincent, get ready for the night of your life! The circus has every cool thing you can think of. First you'll smell the popcorn and hear the big band playing. The ringmaster will come out in a shiny red coat and top hat. In his boomy voice, he'll say stuff like: 'Welcome, ladies and gentleman and children of all ages...'

"Acrobats come tumbling out! They jump and leapfrog, and turn somersaults and cartwheels. They spin hoops on their arms and legs. The jugglers toss rings and balls and all kinds of stuff in the air and everyone parades around in their sparkly costumes.

"Then the music gets all mysterious. The lights lower almost to darkness. A blue mist creeps in and fills the ring. All of a sudden, two white horses charge out of the darkness, their flowing manes shimmering in the misty fog! They rear up on their hind legs and dance around their trainer.

"The lights go up and the music gets faster. The horses break into a speedy gallop around the ring, jumping through hoops that get higher and higher! More horses come out, with riders on them. The riders do flips off of the horses, each one landing on the horse behind her!

"The lights get low again. The music changes. The spotlight moves up, up, up, to the highwire! A woman tiptoes across.

"She stands on one leg...she does a split on the wire! A man walks out onto the wire too. He does jumps and scissor-kicks. He does a backwards somers—"

"Do they ever fall off?" Vincent urgently whispered.

"Oh, sure. That's what makes the circus so dangerous and exciting."

Vincent nervously bit his lip.

Danny said, "I'm just kidding you, buddy. They almost never fall off. They're real pros."

Vincent let out a big breath.

"What else? What else?!" he begged.

"Let's see. There's the dogs! Yeah, the dogs do some really cool tricks.

"And the clowns! The clowns are awesome! Some walk on stilts so they look about as tall as a house. Others ride super-high unicycles or drive these wacky little cars or throw pies at each other.

"The acrobats are really cool, too! They hang from rings and twist their bodies up like pretzels. Then, on the ground, two of them clasp their arms together and toss their brother up into the air. He does somersaults in the air, then comes back and lands in their arms. They throw him up again, and he lands on his brother's shoulders. Then they each flip themselves up on top of the top guy's shoulders until they're a big human totem pole!

"And wait till you see the bears in their tutus! The dancing bears will crack you up! Some of them ride motorcycles and do wheelies..."

"What about the elephants?!" asked Vincent. He was so
wound up, he could barely spit the words out. "What do
the elephants do?"

"Well, they dance ballet for one thing! They stand up on their hind legs and carry people around in their mouths. The coolest part is when an elephant holds a girl by his trunk and spins her around really fast.

"And the trapeze artists! They really fly! One swings across on a trapeze, then lets go. Another one catches her legs and swings her upside down. Then he lets go and she does a somersault in mid-air! She switches trapezes with a new guy who's just swung in. Then, blindfolded, the new guy does a triple somersault!"

Danny's father bought their tickets and said, "Ready, sport?"

"Wait, Dad," said Danny. Then, to Vincent, he said, "But that's not even the best. The best, the very coolest act in the circus is: THOR! Wait till you see this giant cat in action!"

Vincent's eyes were as big and round as saucers. "This is gonna be the best birthday present I ever got!" he yelled.

Vincent hopped up and down with excitement as his dad stepped up to the window. The ticket agent shook her head. "I'm sorry, sir. The management doesn't accept this coupon anymore. You'll have to pay full price."
Vincent's father stood still.

In a small voice, Vincent said, "What's the matter, Dad? Buy the tickets!"

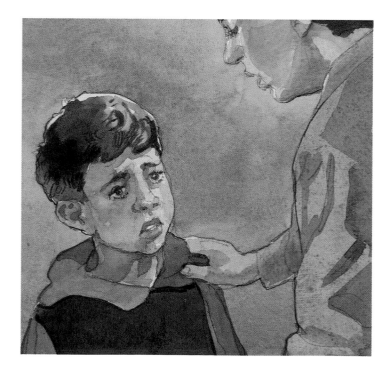

He doesn't have the money, Danny thought. His heart sank as Vincent's father closed his wallet and gently pulled Vincent out of the line. Vincent wouldn't see the circus. All of Danny's excitement melted away until he felt like crying. He looked up at his dad and whispered, "What can we do?"

Danny's father thought for a moment, then said, "You know, the courts are open late tonight, Son. Would you rather see the same old circus again, or shoot some hoops instead?" He handed Danny the two tickets he had just bought, saying, "It's up to you."

Danny understood right away. He thought about the decision his father was letting him make.

A warm, good feeling filled Danny up inside, and a smile crept across his face. "I guess I could use some practice for Saturday's game," he said.

Vincent and his father were already walking away.

"Hey, Vincent," Danny called, running to them.

Vincent turned around, wiping his nose on his sleeve. "What?" he mumbled.

Danny saw the tear streaks on Vincent's face and for a moment he didn't know what to say.

"I really liked telling you about the circus, buddy. And I guess... I want you to see it more than I want to see it myself. I've got this basketball game... Anyway, my dad and I are going to go practice, so it turns out we don't need these tickets after all. Really." Danny held the tickets out to Vincent.

Vincent's face lit up like Christmas. "Can we, Dad?"

Vincent's father looked at Danny with eyes full of thanks. Before the man could say anything, Danny pressed the tickets into Vincent's hand and ran back to his own dad.

Danny's father knelt down and hugged Danny hard. He said, "You did a very kind and special thing tonight, Son. I'm so proud of you."

They didn't see the circus, but to Danny, it was the best night out with Dad ever.